NANNIES for HIRE

Amy Hest

NANNIES

for

HIRE

illustrations by Irene Trivas

MORROW JUNIOR BOOKS ▪ NEW YORK

For a couple of world-class friends,
Kate and Ryan
— A. H.

Pen and ink with watercolor and gouache paints were used for the full-color artwork.
The text type is 15-point Tiffany Light.

Text copyright © 1994 by Amy Hest
Illustrations copyright © 1994 by Irene Trivas

Printed in Singapore at Tien Wah Press.

1 2 3 4 5 6 7 8 9 10

Library of Congress Cataloging-in-Publication Data
Hest, Amy. Nannies for hire / Amy Hest ; illustrations by Irene Trivas.   p.   cm.
Summary: Three friends, Casey, Jenny, and Kate, are excited when Jenny's
mother has a baby and they decide to go to work as nannies.
ISBN 0-688-12527-1. — ISBN 0-688-12528-X (lib. bdg.)
[1. Babies—Fiction.   2. Babysitters—Fiction.   3. Friendship—Fiction.]
I. Trivas, Irene, ill.   II. Title.   PZ7.H4375Nar
1994   [E]—dc20   93-7040   CIP   AC

Contents

Hello Reader!

I now present, for your reading pleasure, the true story of three good friends and how they became nannies for hire. (In case you are wondering about the word *nanny,* I'm not talking about a goat, a grandmother, or someone's old aunt. It's a person who guards a baby.)

Now I will introduce the friends. Me first—Casey. Then Jenny Marks. And last but not least, Kate. In fact, Kate is my real best friend, but whenever someone says it, Jenny has a fit. Sometimes she cries. So Kate and I mostly keep it secret. I swear, we hardly ever say a word.

 The News of the Decade

It all started with Jenny's mother, whose name is Mrs. Marks. She has a first name, too, which is Mindy, but we aren't allowed to call her that. Well, one day she just got fat! I am telling you the truth. The day before, she looked regular. That was the day Jenny's parents said these exact words to her, and I quote:

"Guess what, darling girl! *You are going to be a sister!*"

"Me?" Jenny's hand went straight to her heart. "I am?"

3

"We know you're thrilled," they said. "We know our Jenny is not the kind of girl who worries about things like will we love a cute little precious baby more than we love her."

Then Jenny's father went off to work, and Jenny's mother whipped out a picture book all about having a baby. "We'll read a chapter a night," she said, "and you can ask me anything you want." Mrs. Marks pulled on her planting gloves. She picked up her planting spoon and put on her old straw hat. Then she tripped out to the terrace to check her tomatoes.

Jenny couldn't wait to tell.

"Major family news!" she whispered into the telephone. "Come on up to my place, now!"

"What about Kate?"

"She's on her way." Jenny hung up. I was a little mad she called Kate first, but I was curious, too, so I charged up the back stairs.

"Mrs. Marks is going to have a baby!" blabbed Kate.

"*You* weren't supposed to tell," Jenny said. "It's *my* mother."

"It just came out." Kate was doing a dance across the kitchen floor. *Shuffle step, shuffle step.* Now that she takes tap two days a week instead of one like the rest of us, Kate might be going professional.

5

"You know," I said, "babies really like me." It was a funny thing to say because I couldn't remember the last time I talked to a live baby that wasn't a doll. "When do we get to see yours? What's its name?"

"I forgot to ask," Jenny said.

"All my life I wanted a sister called Bonnie." Double shuffle, turn around, *step step*. "Carmen is a good name, too. Carmen Cassandra Marks!" Kate kept going. "Or maybe you guys like the *M*'s…Melinda, Miranda, Melissa….How about Wendy?"

"It might be a boy baby," I said.

Jenny shook her head. "This family does not need a boy baby. I am not entirely sure we need a baby at all."

"I wish we had one in my house," said Kate. "All we have is me."

"Better tell your mom to read this." Jenny plopped her new book on the counter.

We looked at every picture. Then we started all over.

"Somebody made it up," said Kate after

awhile. "This book has nothing to do with a person's parents." Her face was red. Jenny's was red, too.

    We stuffed it in a brown bag. Jenny shoved the bag way up on a high shelf next to *The Tomato Lover's Cookbook*. What else can you do with a book like that?

2 Introducing Baby . . . and the Boss of Babies

Daisy Lisa Marks arrived in a snowstorm. She had no hair and a wrinkled face, but the minute I saw her, I wanted a baby just like her. I decided to take it up with my mother.

"Babies are extremely cute people," I said.

"I know all about it." She kicked off her working-mother shoes and headed for the kitchen to start dinner.

"I bet you miss having a baby to cuddle." I watched her wash lettuce. "Mrs.

Marks says I can cuddle Daisy anytime I want."

My mother popped a cherry tomato in her mouth.

"Did you know modern babies wear these snappy little suits with feet," I said, "so their toes don't get cold?"

"*You* looked best in blue. Everyone

thought you were a boy." My mother put on her remembering expression. Whenever she does that, you think she's going to cry. "Syd wore pink....What a princess...."

"Syd wore pink suits with feet?"

My mother put lettuce in the spinner. She sighed. I bet she was thinking the same thing I was. I bet she was thinking, How could a princess like my sister, Syd, turn into a monster teenager who loves loud music, wild parties, and nightly calls to her ten best friends?

That was the end of our little talk.

Kate and I went to Jenny's house before school.

"Where is she?" we asked.

"Shhh." Jenny put a finger to her lips. "Daisy is not what you would call a morning person. She is a *night* person who stays up all night." Jenny made a grunting noise.

"Can we see her?"

"Not a chance! There is nothing quite as beautiful as a sleeping baby." That was Mr. Marks, who looked the way my father does when he forgets to shave on Sunday. Anyway, Mr. Marks is famous for his boysenberry pancakes, and he was making stacks of them. I never saw a person yawn so much or make so many pancakes.

11

We went to Jenny's house after school.

Daisy Lisa was all snuggled up in a blanket in Mrs. Marks's lap. One tiny foot stuck out.

"Can I touch her toes?" I whispered.

Jenny looked surprised. "Only people with the last name Marks are allowed to touch her toes," she whispered back.

"Can I give Daisy a bottle?" I asked out loud. "I know how."

"When she's bigger, you may." Mrs. Marks's eyelids drooped, but she smiled in a very kind way.

"Would you like me to sing a lullaby?" asked Kate. "I can sing and tap at the same time."

"A lullaby sounds lovely," said Mrs. Marks.

"No tap?" Kate looked hurt.

"Next time, maybe."

So Kate sang a little song, making up the words as she went along. Her song was about a baby named Bonnie who stayed up all night, counting stars. Kate's voice is soft and sweet. In less than a minute, Mrs. Marks was sound asleep. You can always tell when grown-ups are sleeping sitting up because their mouths pop open and their heads roll to one side.

"Hurry!" whispered Jenny. "You may touch her toes!"

So we each chose a toe, and the one I touched felt like a piece of velvet.

Mrs. Marks made a little snorting sound.

"You may return tomorrow," Jenny said. "After school is best."

"I can teach her to tap." Kate smiled at the thought of it.

"Can I give her a bath?" I asked. "I know how."

"You may watch," said Jenny, the boss of babies. "If you watch me, you will learn a lot."

14

Kate's Big Idea

A long time later Daisy was six months old. On the first day of summer vacation, Kate called a meeting. Kate likes meetings, and she likes to be in charge.

"This meeting is all about sharing," she said. "Three good friends ought to share *everything*."

I was thinking about my new marker set from Grampa. I was thinking maybe I should hide my favorite marker, peacock blue.

"You know," Kate went on, "there's only

one person here with a baby. It's not fair."

"You're absolutely right." Jenny yawned. "It's *not* fair."

"Tired?" Kate asked. "Parents cranky?" She clicked her tongue. "Mom says they were cranky for a whole *year* after I was born."

"Babies are so much trouble!" Jenny groaned. "Especially the ones who take over your room. They cry. They spit up and smell bad. One baby I know burps like a man. If you change this baby's diaper every hour, it's not enough. If you pick her up, she wants down. If you put her down, she wants up." Once she started, it was like Jenny couldn't stop. "And *nobody* pays attention to normal-size girls when there's a baby in the house!" She started to cry.

"Daisy burps like a man?" I was hoping one day she would do it for me.

Jenny sniffled.

Kate was tapping all around the dining room. Kate's dining room has six chairs but no table due to the fact that her mother

spends more time typing than shopping. She says she is writing a best-seller.

"Your family needs help." Kate tried a split. She got about halfway down. "I have a plan. We, meaning three good friends, *we* shall take care of Daisy."

"We shall?" I squeaked. "After everything she just said?"

"Big sisters always say mean things about little sisters," said Kate.

"Not Syd," I lied. "She thinks I'm great."

"The plan has three parts. One." Kate held up a finger. "We take care of Daisy. Finally, Mrs. Marks gets a baby break. She can plant tomatoes on the terrace. She can plant beans the way she used to, or maybe carrots. So"—Kate took a breath—"Mrs. Marks is happy. Are you with me so far?"

"With you."

"Two." Kate held up two fingers. "Mr. Marks comes home from the office. What does he find? A happy wife. So *he's* happy. Which brings us to part three." She waved three fingers. "When there are two happy grown-ups in the house, they can finally pay attention to their normal-size girl. They can pay attention to their Jenny!"

"Wow." Jenny glowed.

"Our services are free of charge?" I asked.

"Not a chance." Kate drew dollar signs in the air.

We found her mother typing the best-seller.

"Do you know another word that means *baby-sitter*?" Kate's mother knows a lot of big words. Little ones, too.

18

"Let me think....There's *nurse*...*nursemaid*...*governess*....In India they say *ayah*....The English like *nanny*...."

We took a vote on the best thing to call ourselves. I liked *baby-sitter* because it was plain. Jenny kept bowing. "I am *ayah*," she said. "I am the great and wonderful *ayah*...." Kate thought *nanny* was best because it sounded proper.

Kate got her way, since it was her mother who knew all the words. But Jenny made the sign.

 ## How to Handle a Baby

We found Mrs. Marks slumped across the kitchen table. You couldn't see her face, but we knew who it was. Daisy was sacked out in her baby swing.

"Nannies for hire!"

Jenny's mother jumped.

"Nannies for hire!"

Jenny's mother looked weird. Her eyes were slightly crossed, and her hair looked like orange toothpicks standing up in a lot of directions.

"Help is on the way," said Jenny in her child-of-the-month voice.

"How much will it cost me?"

"Each nanny gets paid a dollar an hour." We had voted Kate in charge of finance.

"When can you start?"

"How's tomorrow," I said.

Just then Daisy's eyes popped open.

Mrs. Marks stood up. "If you start right now, meaning right this minute, I will pay double."

And so it began.

Mrs. Marks taped a bunch of rules to the refrigerator door. It was mostly a list of things *not* to do. It took up a whole page, then half of another.

"Ready, nannies?"

"Ready," we said.

"Then *adios* and *au revoir!*" Mrs. Marks blew kisses. "Remember"—she turned halfway—"I'm right out here if you need me." She put on her baseball cap and picked up her planting tools. She slid open the terrace door, then let it slide shut.

Daisy had dozed off again. Her chubby baby chest went up and down. Her lips were little rosebud lips, all puckered up like they were waiting for a kiss.

"Look at this perfect angel," I said.

"She is only perfect when she sleeps," Jenny said. "Except sometimes in the bath. She loves to splash around."

"Let's give her a bath," I said. "I know how."

We checked Mrs. Marks's list. The first thing on it was *No Baths!*

Kate was working on her *Who Does What* chart.

```
FOOD AND BEVERAGES................KATE
ENTERTAINMENT......................CASEY
DIAPERS..............................JENNY
```

"*I* do entertainment," Jenny said. "*Casey* does diapers."

"Not me," I said. "The chart says *diapers....Jenny.*"

"Then change the chart. Kate can do diapers, and I'll do food and beverages."

"What kind of nannies are you?" said Kate.

"I'm a no-diaper nanny." I was beginning to wonder when Daisy would wake up.

"Wake up, Daisy!" I whispered, and tickled her toes. "Daisy-girl, time to wake up!" I shuffled my feet on the tile floor.

"Daisy Lisa Marks, you are going to get the most-boring-baby-in-the-world award if you don't wake up!" I pretended to sneeze. Then Kate really did sneeze.

Daisy woke up.

She looked at me in a very unfriendly way.

So I smiled my nicest smile. I was just about to say something loving and sweet, such as "How are you doing, angel?" when Daisy opened her mouth, wide. She opened it so wide, I could see right down to her tonsils. Then she cried, and I am talking *loud.*

Mrs. Marks looked up.

"Everything's fine!" called Kate through the glass door. "Nannies for hire!" She ran to the refrigerator. "*If the baby cries,*" she read, "*check diaper.*"

Nobody moved.

Kate raised her voice. "Check diaper!"

"I vote Casey," said Jenny, "because she wanted Daisy to wake up in the first place."

"I vote Jenny," I said, "because it's *her* sister."

Kate folded her arms. She put on her thinking expression. "You know," she said, "Jenny is the only nanny with experience. We can all learn from someone like that."

You have to admit, Kate knows just what to say, and also when to say it.

So Jenny changed the first diaper, while Kate and I watched from across the room that used to be Jenny's private, no-baby room.

Jenny's old dresser had a million things on it. For example, stacks of diapers. Wiping things. Creamy things. Powder things.

Off in a corner was a tall pink pail.

Jenny took off the old diaper.

I pinched my nose with two fingers. Kate did it, too.

"I'm going to time you." Kate checked her watch. "You may begin!"

Jenny used the wiping things and creamy things.

"Four minutes!" called Kate.

Jenny looked hot. Mad, too. Not Daisy,
though. She was having a grand old time.
Kicking her chubby legs. Swinging her
chubby arms. Cooing and gurgling.

"Jenny does excellent work," said Kate.
"Six minutes!"

"I need a nanny to sprinkle the
powder!"

Kate nudged me with her elbow. I sprinkled.

"Someone open the pail!" Jenny picked up the dirty diaper.

"The nanny who changes the diaper has to open the pail," I said.

Jenny looked me in the eye. "You're next," she said.

 ## *Lunch and Other Disasters*

"I'm in charge of lunch," said Kate.

"Good luck." Jenny smiled.

Here's what happened when the nannies served lunch.

The second Kate put Daisy in the high chair, she cried. Kate said she was spoiled. Jenny said she was hungry. I said Daisy cried because she saw what was coming, meaning homemade baby food.

Now, the easiest thing in the world is to buy baby food. Everybody knows that. Except Mrs. Marks, who believes in *blending* everything fresh for Daisy. Take it from me, all that blending gives the kitchen a bad smell, and anyway, the baby food she makes looks like somebody already ate it.

Kate sniffed the jar. "You give this stuff to a human?" she said.

Jenny nodded. "Poor old Daisy doesn't know better."

Daisy had a whole wardrobe of bibs. I chose the monkey bib. Daisy pulled it off. I put it on. Daisy pulled it off. I put it on. Daisy let it drop to the floor, and that's where it stayed.

"Spoon." Kate held her hand straight out.

Jenny backed up.

"I have right here, for your dining pleasure, a delicious lunch." Kate dipped the spoon into green slime. "Look what your mommy made just for you!" Kate aimed. Daisy opened her button mouth. Her eyes were glued to Kate's face. One little tooth was sticking up on the bottom. Kate moved the spoon, but Daisy moved faster. Lips together!

"No green slime for Daisy!" I cheered. "Smart kid!"

Kate turned on the charm. "Look, angel! Chopped green mush for our little Daisy-girl!" She took aim. Daisy opened her mouth. Kate made a move. Daisy moved faster. Lips together!

"Next time, try diapers," Jenny said.

Kate took a deep breath. "Okay, Daisy-baby. Here goes. I am going to sing you a little song, and when I'm finished, you will eat your delicious green gunk like a good girl. Here's the song:

> "I know a little baby,
>   Her name is bonnie Daisy.
>   Now this may sound crazy,
>   But when bonnie Daisy gets lazy
>   She eats green mush!"

Daisy liked the song. You could tell because she smacked her lips and made humming noises. She banged her fists on

the high chair. Then she grabbed the jar
from Kate and whipped her lunch across the
room. I'm telling you the truth, that stuff flew!
　"Sponge!" cried Jenny. "Paper towels!"
　We found Daisy's lunch everywhere.
Under the high chair and on it. Under the

kitchen counter and on it. There was even a
blob on the glass door clear across the room.
We wiped it out of Daisy's hair, then Kate's.
Everything smelled bad, and everyone.

Daisy never did eat lunch.

I guess she wasn't that hungry.

6 And Now . . . the Littlest Angel

"Entertainment time!" Finally it was my turn to be in charge of something. "Okay, you guys, I'm going to cheer you up with a story."

Now I'm not boasting when I say this, but stories are my specialty. I read them. I tell them. I write them. I draw them.

"Don't make it scary," Kate warned. "Baby on board."

I put Daisy in her baby stroller. I wanted to tell the story out in the park, but of course, there was a *Don't take Daisy to the park!* rule. So instead, I pushed her from one room to the other, and all the time I was pushing, I was talking.

This is the story I told.

"Once upon a time there was a little baby named Vanessa. Vanessa was a royal princess—the real thing—and she lived in a castle high on a hill near the Hudson River. She lived there with her mother and father and seventeen brothers and sisters."

"Seventeen?" Kate and Jenny were skipping after us.

"No interruptions." I pushed the stroller all around the living room and through the dining room, then back to the kitchen. "And all those brothers and sisters were extremely mean. Except for the one called Casey."

"Except for the one called *Jenny,*" Jenny said.

"The nice one is Casey." I squeezed between two tables, then headed into the hallway.

"That's not fair!" Jenny blocked the entrance to her bedroom. "Her name should be Jenny!"

"The nanny who tells the story makes up the names!" I backed out. "And in this story, the good sister is called Casey."

"You could call her Wendy," said Kate.

"It's a bad story," Jenny said.

"Daisy likes it. Right, Daisy-girl?"

Daisy cooed. Her thumb was in her mouth. So was a corner of the baby blanket.

I kept going. "So Princess Vanessa was all set to run away from the castle. Of course, she would take her favorite sister, Casey."

Daisy started to cry.

"Quit making my sister cry," Jenny said.

I pushed the stroller faster. Daisy cried harder. "All *right*. I'll call the good sister Jenny," I said. "But there's another good sister, too, and *her* name is going to be Casey!"

Daisy howled away.

"Maybe I should do a little dance to go with your story," shouted Kate.

"Daisy is not interested in tap," Jenny shouted back.

Kate sighed. Then Jenny. Or maybe it was me. All I know is, my arms hurt from pushing and pulling. My mouth was dry from telling a story that no one liked but me. I was hungry because we didn't get lunch. I smelled like homemade baby food, and I wanted a bath. To tell you the truth, I was getting tired of guarding Daisy. I was tired of being a nanny.

"Nannies! I'm home!" Mrs. Marks whirled in from the terrace. She kept on kissing the side of Daisy's neck. I guess when it's your baby, you don't mind if it smells like green gunk. "How's my little angel? I missed her so much! Hello, baby!"

Wouldn't you know, Daisy quit crying the *second* her mother picked her up. I didn't think that was fair.

"How about a baby break for my wonderful nannies?" Mrs. Marks peeled six dollar bills from a pile of them. "But don't go too far. I'm hoping to hire you again. Soon."

"How soon?" Jenny sounded weak, and Kate looked scared.

Mrs. Marks smiled. "How about tomorrow?" She carried Daisy off to the bedroom. "Be here at noon!"

The nannies made themselves the
biggest ice-cream soda you can imagine.
They each took a straw and a spoon with a
tall handle. And they drank and slurped until
there was nothing in the glass.